John Bascom, Arthur Latham Perry, Austin Bradley Bassett

A Tribute to the Memory of Joseph White

John Bascom, Arthur Latham Perry, Austin Bradley Bassett

A Tribute to the Memory of Joseph White

ISBN/EAN: 9783337340391

Printed in Europe, USA, Canada, Australia, Japan

Cover: Foto ©Raphael Reischuk / pixelio.de

More available books at **www.hansebooks.com**

A Tribute to the Memory of Joseph White.

CONTENTS.

THE LIFE OF JOSEPH WHITE WITH ITS HISTORIC ANTECEDENTS.

Joseph White sprang from a reputable and influential family, earliest settled in the middle valley of the Deerfield River. Capt. Moses Rice, born in Sudbury, October 27, 1694, himself a great-grandson of Edmund Rice, who emigrated from Berkhamstead, in Hertfordshire, England, and settled in Sudbury in 1638, was a great-great-grandfather of Joseph White. Capt. Rice, then a resident of Rutland, in the County of Worcester, purchased two thousand two hundred and fifty acres of land in April, 1741, lying along the Deerfield River in the present town of Charlemont. These lands lay on the north bank of the river, partly meadow and partly upland, and the present road from Deerfield to the Hoosac Tunnel runs through their entire length.

In the spring of 1743, Moses Rice came to his purchase in the primeval forest, preparatory to settling upon it with his family; and the huge buttonwood growing by the roadside is still pointed out, under which, according to the statement of his son, Sylvanus Rice, and handed down to us by the latter's daughter, the late Mrs. Fuller, *"he had slept under the buttonwood tree when there was no other white person in town."* His first low cabin, when builded near the buttonwood, of logs felled by his own strong arm, was the very first erected between Deerfield and the Hoosac Mountain; and his wife and five minor children when gathered beneath the roof-tree, such as it was, were the first family to lift the voice of industry and the notes of prayer and praise in the whole stretch of that winding valley, now so beautiful in its green meadows and so strong in its guardian hills.

The next year after Capt. Rice had set up his household gods on the river bank, Col. Timothy Dwight of Northampton, under the military direction of Gov. Shirley, and in prospect of the war with France, which was proclaimed at Boston in June, ran as a surveyor an east and west line from the Connecticut River at Northfield through Colerain to the Hoosac Mountain for a cordon of forts to protect the Deerfield valley and the Connecticut against the French and Indians. During that summer of 1744, and on Dwight's line, were built Fort Shirley in the present town of Heath, and Fort Pelham in the present town of Rowe, both of them about four miles north of the Deerfield, and each of them built on brooks running parallel about four miles apart down to the Deerfield. The construction of these forts, under the immediate orders of Col. John Stoddard of Northampton, made Capt. Rice an important person in their neighborhood, and his house an important stopping-place for officers and soldiers on their way to and from the forts, because it was then the only house west of Deerfield along that river. Indeed, Stoddard had made a contract with Rice to draw the timbers for one of the forts to the place of construction ; but as the latter failed in some points to come to time, and as the former was a remarkably prompt man, both forts were actually constructed under the immediate direction of William Williams, afterwards the patriarch of Pittsfield.

Still, Rice was constantly trusted by Gov. Shirley and his military subordinates throughout that war, and his house was the rendezvous for everybody concerned in the public events of that region. Rice himself and his sons were at times soldiers for considerable intervals in one or other of the two forts above him on the uplands; and Capt. Ephraim Williams, long time the commandant of the line of forts, and afterwards the founder of Williams College, was often sheltered under that roof as he passed from Shirley and Pelham forts to Fort Massachusetts and back again. Chaplain John Norton has the following entry in his diary: "Thursday, August 14, 1746, I left Fort Shirley in company with Dr. Thomas Williams, and about fourteen of the soldiers; we went to Pelham Fort, and from thence to Capt. Rice's, where we lodged that night."

The good chaplain reached Fort Massachusetts the next day, where he "designed to have tarried about a month;" but the fort was almost immediately invested by a large force of French and Indians, who compelled its surrender on the 20th, burned it to the ground, and carried its garrison (chaplain and all) captives to Canada. A part of this hostile force, however, pressed on from the charred site of Fort Massachusetts to Deerfield, burning Rice's house on their way, the only one intervening between the two points. In a petition to the General Court, made six years afterwards, Rice himself described the desolation of his home: "And returning, in order to take care of his things, found his house was burnt, with a good stock of provision therein (or carried away) by the enemy, as was all his household goods, with a considerable parcel of clothing, his stock of cattle, being seven oxen and cows, together with six very good fat hogs, were all killed by the enemy,—his crop of grain, at least three hundred bushel, with all his hay, husbandry tools, and many other things, all destroyed—his loss being at least fifteen hundred pounds, old tenor."

In the same petition Capt. Rice described his general position during that war, as follows: "That his living was of great service, as he humbly apprehends, to the public, as being the only house where people could be supplied; and, as soldiers were often traveling that way, as well as small parties of scouts, it was very expensive to your petitioner, who often supplied them at his own costs."

After the peace of Aix la Chapelle, Capt. Rice, who in the meantime had gone back to Rutland with his family, returned to his desolated homestead on the Deerfield, rebuilt his house upon the same site, and continued the chief man in the now increasing settlement, until in the next and last French and Indian war, on the 11th of June, 1755, Capt. Rice, with his son, Artemas Rice, and grandson, Asa Rice, with several others, was hoeing corn in his meadow just south of the present village road, when a party of six Indians concealed by the brushwood of a brook, suddenly fired upon and then rushed upon the working party, whose fire-arms had been placed against a pile of logs near by. Phineas Arms fell instantly dead in the cornfield, while Capt. Rice received a severe wound in the thigh, and was taken prisoner with his grandson and one other. The three captives were taken to the high plain in the rear of the present public house in Charlemont Village, where the old man, after a fearful struggle with the single savage to whom he was given over, fell beneath the tomahawk, was scalped, and left bleeding to die after some hours. The other two prisoners were led to Crown Point, and thence to Canada, whence the grandson was ransomed after a captivity of six years; and Titus King, the other, a relative of Capt. Rice, being carried to France and then to England, at length returned to Northampton, his native place.

Joseph White's mother was Rebecca Rice in the direct line, and his childhood and youth in Charlemont was nurtured in all the traditions of this large family, and familiarized with all the geographical localities in which they had lived and wrought for generation after generation. His mind received a color and his character a tone from all these peculiarities of birth and training; the spirit of his educational development and the whole course of his life were altered in consequence of them; and no one could understand Mr. White thoroughly, or comprehend his apparent aberrations from a straightforward career in life, who did not perceive the direction in which his chief intellectual interest lay and the sort of facts which easiest and most permanently roused his emotions. As the centennial of the Charlemont massacre approached, it was determined by him and by Mr. O. B. Potter of New York, his own cousin on the Rice side, that there should be an historical commemoration of Capt. Moses Rice on the anniversary of the fateful day, June 11, 1855, and of his compeers also, in the original plantation of Charlemont; and that an elaborate monument should be erected and publicly dedicated over his grave and that of Phineas Arms killed by the same Indian volley, while at the same time it was wisely decided to allow the rude but enduring contemporary headstones to remain in their place by the side of the monument.

It naturally fell to Mr. White to prepare and deliver the historical discourse upon that interesting occasion. It was a labor of love. It fell in with the deepest currents of his being, both intellectual and religious. He took time for its preparation, which was thoroughly done. He searched the archives in the Secretary's office at Boston, and was rewarded by the discovery of precious documents,

2

which he knew how to interpret, whose significance he inwrought with the results of other careful investigations, and with the siftings of tenacious memories, his own and hosts of others, into a permanent and eloquent chronicle, which remains as his most vital and valuable contribution to the literature of his time.

Of scarcely less consequence to his life and labors than this Rice genealogy in which he stood, was the bit of heredity connecting him in the direct line with John White, who emigrated early from the west of England with his two sons, Josiah and Thomas, and settled in Lancaster, Massachusetts. A great-grandson of this first immigrant was Jonathan (Col.), born at Lancaster, March 31, 1709. Here he became a prominent actor in all enterprises for the public good—in establishing schools; in building a house for public worship, and settling a minister; and in organizing a church, of which he was chosen the first deacon in 1743. Wilder's "History of Lancaster" says of him: "Col. Jonathan White was the greatest landholder, the most wealthy man, the best educated person then in town and a perfect gentleman of those days."

This Col. Jonathan White held the commission of Major, and afterwards that of Lieutenant-Colonel, in Col. Timothy Ruggles' regiment of "New Levies," which marched against Crown Point under Sir William Johnson in the summer of 1755; and was present with his regiment at the so-called "Battle of Lake George," September 8th of that year, in which the French general commanding, Baron de Dieskau, was defeated and taken prisoner. In this battle Ruggles' officers and men fought alongside the officers and men of the regiment of Col. Ephraim Williams, the founder of Williams College, although the brave Colonel himself had been killed that morning in the so-called "bloody morning scout" about two miles south of Lake George. The fact that his great-grand-father fought in that battle, and that the sword he wore at that time finally descended to him, of course early interested Joseph White in that campaign, and in all the combatants in it. He became interested as a boy in Williams College in consequence; still more interested as a student, a tutor, an alumnus, a trustee; and when the centennial of the death of Col. Williams came round, also in the year 1855, there was no other one of their number so intelligent and everyway competent as he, whom the Alumni could appoint to deliver their commem-orative oration upon the founder of the college. Next to his discourse at Charlemont, his effort here the same summer proved to be his most eloquent and permanent contribution to the literature of his time. Mr. White was always a natural orator; partly because his emotional nature was quick and strong in its action, partly because he was painstaking in his preparation, and partly, too, because he had a penetrating instinct as to the popular tastes and interests.

Col. Jonathan White's Lake George sword passed to his son, Col. Asaph White, and then to *his* son, Capt. Joseph White, and finally to *his* son, Mr. Joseph White; who, having no children, thoughtfully presented it to Wil-liams College, in whose historical museum in Clark Hall it is exhibited alongside the sword of Col. Williams him-self, found on his person the next morning after the fight, and the sword also of Col. Thomas Williams, uterine brother of Ephraim, who succeeded to the command of his regiment at Lake George.

In Mr. White's childhood and youth in Charlemont, not only were the traditions of the old French wars lively, and located both personally and geographically, but still more so in both respects the traditions of the Revolutionary War. Col. Hugh Maxwell of Charlemont was eight years in the service without a break, much of the time as the right-hand-man of Gen. Heath, after whom the new township set off from the old by Maxwell's efforts in 1785 was named, and is still called "Heath." Maxwell's descendants were still the leading people of the town at its centennial celebration in 1885. Capt. Oliver Avery also, with thirty-four men from Charlemont and eighteen from Rowe, marched to Cambridge immediately after the engagements at Concord and Lexington, and the company served throughout the war. Of this number was Josiah Pierce, who fired at the enemy in the Bunker's Hill battle, forty-seven bullets, with an unerring aim which was proverbial in his time, and who lived to tell and retell his own and others' exploits till the middle of the present century. Ebenezer Fales was killed in that battle, and Hugh Maxwell dangerously wounded.

Mr. White's own grandfather, Samuel Rice, was a scarred veteran of the Revolution, and lived to pour into the eager ears of his grandson tales of his own sufferings in and escape from captivity in Canada,—tales also of what he saw with his own eyes and heard with his own ears. He witnessed the quarrel between Ethan Allen and Benedict Arnold on the east brink of Lake Champlain in the gray of the morning of May 10, 1775, when Arnold claimed precedence at the head of the column about to enter the fortress of Ticonderoga; Allen had the best right, and the men who had followed him so far, forty-one of them men of Williamstown and Hancock under Israel Harris, insisted that they would follow no other in the approaching attack on the Fort; Arnold yielded to the inevitable, but with a very bad grace; for Samuel Rice used to say, that Arnold at this point struck Allen a heavy blow on the shoulder with the flat of his sword, so that the scabbard slipped off into the water; and when the Charlemont boy expressed dilated surprise that Allen did not resent such an insult, the rejoinder was: "*Allen hadn't got no grit, Joe!*"

This Samuel Rice, like his neighbor, Hugh Maxwell, suffered fearfully from the inconvertible Continental money. The war was over, the money was worthless, and the returned veterans were heavily in debt. The courts were opened again, civil process against debtors began to be enforced by the sheriff and his deputies, and the movement in Western Massachusetts, that later came to a head under Daniel Shays, was stirring the hearts of all the old soldiers. Debts contracted to support the mother and the children, while the father was away in the war, hung over his little property when he returned, unpaid. Legal process was resorted to to collect them. The deputy-sheriff, who was an old friend of the veteran, came to the cabin with the warrant in his hands to attach it, and its contents. Rice was a carpenter by trade, and he took his stand in the open door, with his broad-ax in his powerful right hand, and thus accosted the deputy as he approached to enter: "*I've known ye long, and I love ye like a brother, but if ye try to cross this threshold, I'll split ye from your crown to your heels!*"

"And he would have done it, too," was the usual comment of the grandson as he related the incident. Such associations as these with persons, and especially with family and local traditions, gave a permanent bent to the boy's mind, and to the favorite studies of a lifetime. He gradually became fond of biography and history; he burrowed in his leisure in the records of the old French Wars; he became very familiar with the revolutionary campaigns, especially at the northward, and with the pre-revolutionary and post-revolutionary heroes generally; and he slowly acquired what came to be by far the most valuable private library in Williamstown, being particularly rich in the special lines but just now indicated.

When he was sixteen years old, he made his first visit to Williamstown. His father, Capt. Joseph White, was a cloth-dresser, who drew his customers from a very wide circuit. He had done work, for example, for the Smedleys, at that time an important family here; and the boy crossed the mountain on horseback by the present road, which had been laid out and built by his grandfather, Col. Asaph White, with a message to the Smedleys that assured him of hospitality over the commencement of 1827. That was a somewhat famous commencement, on two grounds. The graduating class consisted of twenty-six men, sixteen of them being among the founders and members of the "Williams College Temperance Society," whose constitution and membership have been fortunately preserved to us. Eleven out of the eighteen members of the class of 1828 belonged to it, thirteen out of twenty-one of the class of 1829 also, and ten out of twenty-eight of the class of 1830. Temperance, then a newly organized thing in New England, prominently appeared on the commencement stage in 1827, especially in the "Colloquy," in which Asahel Foote displayed remarkable powers of irony and sarcasm, which not only took mightily with the audience, including the boy White, but also is said to have visibly shaken the sides of the gigantic President Griffin, extra dignified in his cap and gown. Young White had secured an early seat in the gallery, which he only quitted at the noon intermission long enough to secure a cake of gingerbread for his dinner of one of the peddlers, who at that time thronged the space in the rear of the church.

The afternoon furnished him a greater treat still. The valedictory oration and the conferring of the degrees, and particularly the Master's oration, delivered that year by Mark Hopkins, on "Mystery," impressed the boy beyond measure, and made him resolve then and there if it were a possible thing, he would go to college himself. That Master's oration, by the way, published a short time afterwards in "*Silliman's Journal*," in New Haven (Professor Silliman having been present here at that commencement), was the very beginning of the public reputation of Mark Hopkins. Three years later he was appointed Professor of Rhetoric; and in 1836, on the very day when White, in accordance with his purpose formed nine years before, appeared on the commencement stage to speak and to be graduated, was elected by the trustees President of the College. It is very doubtful, however, whether he would have been chosen at that time, had it not been for the class of which White was an influential member. The trustees thought Hopkins too young (he was thirty-four), and elected Absalom Peters president, who declined. This class, who had enjoyed the services of the Professor throughout the senior year in the studies usually taught by Dr. Griffin, as well as in his own, sent in to the trustees a paper in token of their warm approbation of his work in both directions. "*If the boys want him, let 'em have him!*" was the exclamatory word of Dr. Shepard of the trustees, and the body followed suit immediately.

After teaching for a while, one year in the College as a tutor, Mr. White studied law in Troy with M. I. Townsend, W. C. '33, and practiced for some years with his brother-in-law there, A. B. Olin, W. C. '35. But he never took much root as a lawyer. He disliked the manners, the quibbles and the quarrels of the bar. In looking up a case, it was its historical aspect and relations that interested him rather than its purely legal bearings ; and he would sometimes spend days and nights in arduous research into these remoter matters, which, however profitable to himself in the development of his own mind, was the opposite of profitable to his clients and to his partner. Unfortunately, also, he became a popular young Whig orator in the political campaigns of the period. The career of Daniel Webster and of Rufus Choate dazzled him, as it did many other young men of the time to their detriment. The principal stock in trade of the political orators of that decade was the tariff-question, a question of which most of the speakers on both sides were profoundly ignorant, and of which Mr. White in his old age used freely and playfully to acknowledge that he knew absolutely nothing. Still, in this way he became practiced in public-speaking, an art of which he was fond, and in which he became skilled.

Dr. Beaman was the pastor of the First Presbyterian church in Troy while Mr. White was a resident of that city, and the relations between the two men gradually came to be intimate and very helpful to both. The religious character of the younger man rounded out under the stimulating preaching and uplifting impulses generally of the elder one ; and Mr. White fairly entered upon what was the most distinguishing characteristic of his whole life, namely, intelligent fidelity as a layman in all departments of church work, particularly in an earnest and comprehensive study of the Scriptures in relation to and preparation for Bible-class instruction. An excellent portrait of Dr. Beaman has hung for many years in Mr. White's private library, and is hanging there still. No lapse of time ever seemed to obliterate his sense of obligation to this pastor, or to cool his expression of admiration for him.

When Mr. White abandoned the law, and went to Lowell to live as an agent for one of the cotton corporations there, there was no great change in the general tenor of his life. He continued to make upon occasion political speeches for the then and always moribund Whig party, which added little to his reputation, though it offered scope to some exceptionally fine oratorical powers; and he was elected to the State Senate from Lowell for one winter, in which he was colleague with the gentle and genial Dr. Sabin of Williamstown, with whom he had been a colleague in the corporation of the College since 1848, in which capacity they served together till Dr. Sabin's death in 1884. His church and Sunday-school work in Lowell was largely profitable to himself and others. It was apparent already, that his deepest impress upon his generation would be made, as was most fit, at the point of Christian influence and example.

In 1860, Mr. White, who had become secretary and treasurer of the college the year before on the death of Judge Daniel N. Dewey, was made Secretary of the Board of Education of the State of Massachusetts, a place he held for seventeen years. This was a greatly important post, and one difficult to fill after the extraordinary labors of Horace Mann for eleven years, and the striking activity in it of George S. Boutwell. But his lectures as secretary and his teachers' institutes held all over the State, which were always popular and successful, brought into play his early training in extempore speaking, his store of knowl-

3

edge as to the history of Massachusetts, his remarkable familiarity with the biographical details of its great men, and his taste and skill in handling picturesque and illustrative incidents. By much the most successful work of his life was accomplished during these seventeen years. They had their trials and limitations of course, like all other successful human work everywhere. His own quick temper was an infirmity. An indolent habit of mind and body, a native tendency to postpone impending duty, and a consequent facility of throwing off, perhaps at a late hour, upon other shoulders responsibilities which were properly his own, marred more or less during all his later years his services both to the public and the college. His religious life and service, however, knew no intermissions. His faith grew simpler and steadier and stronger as his years increased. His interest in the Bible and his Bible-class diminished not as his years increased. As a deacon in the church, he grew more tender and exemplary, as a constant attendant at the weekly prayer-meeting, his contributions to its spiritual and uplifting power were noticeable and apparently indispensable ; his native imagination, to which he had always given a chastened scope, enabled him to mount up as on eagles' wings, and help to bear others along with him ; and his naturally fervid emotions responded promptly to every spiritual call.

For the last dozen years of his life he frequented with great regularity the quarterly meetings of the Berkshire Historical and Scientific Society at Pittsfield. For three years he was its President. He did his share of its work. His presence there was always a stimulus and a benediction to others ; he could correct their mistakes, upon occasion ; and he appreciated, as few men are able to do, the care and the insight and the vigilence needful to conduct to a successful issue any genuine historical investigation.

In person, Mr. White was tall, symmetrically built, and in his prime strikingly handsome. He took much more than an ordinary gentleman's pains with his personal appearance. He dressed expensively, but never extravagantly. By economy in its best sense he came to possess and enjoy a competent estate. He had no children, and the wife of his youth survives him. He was born at Charlemont, November 18, 1811, and died two or three days after entering his 80th year.

THE LIFE OF JOSEPH WHITE, WITH TRIBUTES OF FRIENDS.

The parentage of Joseph White, the period and place of his birth and his rearing were all fitted to call out patriotism and give the love of country distinct and passionate expression. Charlemont, a secluded village in the midst of bold, beautiful scenery, on the banks of the Deerfield, pouring with unfailing energy through its deep mountain valley, begat and nourished local attachment and the love of nature. Born November 18, 1811, his childhood was but little farther removed from the war of the Revolution than we are from that of the Rebellion. He began to gather the first impressions of life during the second struggle with England. Charlemont, under the shadow of the forts originally designed to protect our northern border, directly felt and fanned the martial sentiment. It had reminiscenses of war which could not but deeply move the restless spirit of a boy. Massachusetts had then many a nook well fitted to grow sturdy men, and Charlemont was manifestly one of them.

Joseph spent his youth within the circle of the influence of Williams College ; and a visit to it one Commencement day awakened a desire which passed into a fixed resolve, to secure a liberal education.

He began to prepare for college, aiding himself by the unfailing resource of school-teaching. He attended for a time the Academy in Bennington, and then entered Williams in the class of '36. His education, the fruit of his own exertions, and received within this well-defined and stirring historic area, served to widen and strengthen his local and civic ties.

Professor John Tatlock and Dr. Crawford of Deerfield, with whom he maintained a warm friendship through life, were his classmates. The three became tutors in the college.

"Though Mr. White's preliminary course had been brief, he made up for it by faithful study, and was early numbered among the best scholars in his class. He was remembered among his fellow-students as staid and dignified, and always on the side of right. He graduated with the first English oration. After leaving College he taught several months in the Seminary at Bennington.

"In March, 1837, he began the study of law in the office of Judge J. D. Willard, of Troy, N. Y., going thence in October following to that of Hon. Martin I. Townsend & Brother, where he remained until January, 1839. He then returned to his Alma Mater as tutor, serving in that office until Commencement of 1840. In 1841, he married Miss Hannah Danforth, of Williamstown, and soon after, returning to Troy, he entered the legal profession in partnership with his brother-in-law, the late Hon. A. B. Olin. This connection continued for several years. While residing in Troy, Mr. White became connected with the Presbyterian church; to this he made himself greatly useful; and to the day of his death he lived a consistent, practical, Christian life. He was liberal toward the faith of others, but devoted and zealous in maintaining and exemplifying his own.

"In December, 1848, he removed to Lowell, Mass., where as agent he took charge of the Massachusetts Cotton Mills, one of the largest manufacturing corporations in New England. Meanwhile he was elected a member of the Massachusetts Senate, serving during the session of 1857, and acting as chairman of two important committees. He was also chairman of a special Committee on Retrenchment and Reform. In 1858 he was appointed Bank Commissioner, which office he resigned in 1860.

"In 1848 Mr. White was elected trustee of Williams College. At Commencement, 1855, he delivered an oration before the Society of Alumni in memorial of the founder, Ephraim Williams. In March, 1859, he was chosen college treasurer. He accepted the position, and on the first of January following removed to Williamstown, where he has since resided.

"In July, 1860, he received the appointment of secretary of the State Board of Education, and continued in the discharge of the very exacting duties of that office until May, 1876, a period of nearly sixteen years. Mr. White was a firm friend of the High Schools, and was instrumental in securing their establishment in many towns; he was heartily opposed to the District system, and secured its first abolition; and when it was again restored, he dealt it hard blows, which had their effect in its final abandonment. He was an earnest advocate for a general tax upon the whole State valuation, for the support, in part, of the public schools. This measure passed the House of of Representatives by a large vote, and only wanted one in the Senate to become a law. Mr. White always kept in mind the needs of the poorer towns of the State, and it was with sad regret that, having remained longer in the office than was his desire, he retired from the secretaryship without securing the passage of this just and beneficent act. He was instrumental in bringing into the schools a system of industrial drawing, and of establishing the Normal Art School, for the training of teachers in the art.

He was a sympathizing friend of the teachers, and always an advocate of advanced methods.

"In 1868, Yale College conferred on him the honorary degree of LL. D. A second time, in 1875, Mr. White served as a member of the State Legislature, and was chairman of the Joint Committee on Education. During recent years he has withdrawn himself from public office, giving his time mainly to his duties in connection with the college at Williamstown and to the management of his farm and home affairs. At the College Commencement in 1886 he resigned his position at treasurer of the college." —*Necrology of Massachusetts Teachers' Association, by Geo. A. Walton.*

Mr. White was closely and widely identified with the interests of education from his youth up. Starting in the ranks as a teacher of a district school, he attained the highest position in public instruction in the gift of the State. He brought to all his work a liberal and progressive spirit. He was closely associated with Williams College as an active trustee for forty-two years ; and also with Smith College from its foundation. Of the latter institution, he was appointed trustee by the donor of its funds, and frequently consulted by her in the formation of plans concerning it. He warmly favored Northampton as the seat of the institution, and was influential in securing that location.

His life was devoted to the service of the public in its most important, though not most conspicuous, interests.

" Mr. White's death is a loss to the community in which he lived, and to Berkshire County and the State. His force of character, high motives and public spirit made him a pillar of strength to society and the church, and a power for good wherever his influence was felt. He was deeply interested in church work at home and also in religious progress throughout the world. His long identification with Williams College made him seem a part of it. He was a close observer of current affairs and every movement for the amelioration and uplifting of the race the world over had his earnest sympathy and support. His life was a blessing to his fellow men and an example well worthy of emulation, and the end was as peaceful as the setting of the sun at the close of a long and perfect day."—*The North Adams Transcript, Nov. 27, 1890.*

His classmate, Dr. Crawford, says of him : " In college Mr. White, like myself and some others of the class, was at first at a disadvantage for want of thorough preparation to begin with. But he was assiduous and persevering in his studies, and notwithstanding we had some strong men among us, he very soon took rank with the first. There, by dint of application, he kept all through the course. True, perhaps, he was not a genius ; he was not specially brilliant in any particular line of studies, but what is better, he was prompt and accurate in them all. And this has been characteristic of him in all the varied positions and offices to which he has been called in subsequent life. Not a genius, not sporadic, he was a man of affairs, having a good judgment, and good, common sense, and the power of adapting himself to new duties and circumstances as they presented themselves. While in college he was highly esteemed by all, both as a scholar and as a man, correct and dignified in his deportment, a pleasant companion, and always on the side of right. He graduated with honor, having the first English oration.

* * * * * * * *

" The life of Mr. White was not one of sloth or easy self-indulgence ; nor was it one of mere self-seeking. He was a busy man, modest and retiring, but self-reliant and industrious. He was careful and saving in personal matters, but lived amply and was nobly generous. Few men during the course of a long life have held so many and important positions, and of such varied character, filling them all with ability and credit, exerting on each an influence healthful and lasting. He was a man of fine presence, a fair and genial countenance, and in his old age venerable with hair silken-white,—one who might well be called 'a gentleman of the old school.' He had a large acquaintance with men, and friendly tact in dealing with them, a high sense of honor and right, and throughout his long and varied career not even the suspicion of a dishonest or dishonorable act ever attached to his name.

"He was greatly influential in his town affairs, took an active part in their management, and was often moderator of the town meeting, having the fullest confidence of his fellow-townsmen of all parties. He had a like standing and interest in church matters ; a devout member of long standing, and for a number of years deacon of the Congregational church, active and useful and to almost the close of his life a teacher of a large adult class in the Sunday school.

"Withal, he was an attractive and elegant speaker, clear and forcible, and specially apt in impromptu efforts. He had made this a study, and his long experience in public life had given him ample opportunity for its practice.

"Mr. White was a good type of the best New England manhood, proud of his origin and belongings, and a loving investigator all his life of New England institutions and history. Few men have been better informed, or could reason more intelligently, with regard to the things which have made the life of this section what it is."

4

My own recollections of Mr. White are almost wholly associated with Williamstown, its college and church, its schools and town affairs. Early in his residence with us, school questions of much moment came before the town for its immediate action. The need of a high-school and a high-school building had become urgent. It was very necessary that the districts should be re-arranged and reduced in number, and that new school houses should be built throughout the town. Worthy and influential citizens were slow to feel the urgency of these demands, and protracted and warm discussion was called out. Mr. White brought his influence to bear powerfully and persuasively in this contest, and the effort was ultimately crowned with complete success.

Mr. White was a man of fine presence, agreeable address, and was an animated and sympathetic speaker. He possessed a mobile, emotional nature which easily came to the surface in speech, and aroused an immediate popular response. The town meetings of Williamstown have been remarkable in this respect. A number of citizens like Mr. White and Dr. Henry L. Sabin and others still with us, have at once invested with importance town affairs of any considerable moment, and have brought to them a surprising pathos. Passing through the valley of Baca, they have made it a well. The word, Berkshire, has had for them as many and as liquid syllables as the word, Jerusalem. The result has been constant, animated and instructive deliberation on the business of the town. "'A community of persons, living within prescribed limits under self-imposed laws,' was to Mr. White a divine institution, and he was averse to all legislation which tended to impair the autonomy of the town." He felt the popular life, believed in the popular life, and did all that he could to expand and improve it. The pictures of memory which most spontaneously arise of him will always be those of the public assemblies in which he so long acted the part of an influential and patriotic citizen. His latter years were marked by failing strength, though he retained, almost to the very end, a comfortable possession of his powers. His death occurred November 30, 1890. The funeral services were held on the following Sunday in the Congregational church under the direction of its pastor, A. B. Bassett, assisted by Dr. Bascom and President Carter.

ADDRESS AT THE FUNERAL BY THE PASTOR.

Two feelings are in all our hearts to-day. Respect for a good citizen and love for a good man have brought us here. In our thought of Mr. White honor and affection blend. Our sense of loss takes color and intensity from both. As his pastor, it is my privilege to remind you of those qualities in him which our love has long since fixed upon and which memory now holds tenaciously; to speak of him as the good man, the Christian, and as an officer in this church. Some thirty years ago Mr. White came permanently into the life of this village in the full maturity of his powers. His practice of law in early manhood, a later business experience, service as a public official and finally as Secretary of the State Board of Education had given him contact with life in many of its phases, a broad interest in the problems of our time and an acquaintance with the ruling principles in national, state and local government. To the town, endeared to him by the associations of his student years, and to the College, which he never ceased to love, he brought his mature wisdom and wholesome influence. Here the fruit of his life ripened, to the profit of this community in its educational, civil and religious interests. Even since the decline of strength in these last years has narrowed his activities, the benignity of his example and his counsel has been felt wherever that courtly figure moved or that magnetic voice was heard. And if I have rightly judged our venerable brother and his influence, his life for the last score of years has been beautiful in a rare degree. "The beauty of the Lord" has been upon it. Life has two periods of beauty. There is a beauty of youth. Hope is on the young man's brow. Fair promises shine from his eye. An eager energy stirs in every nerve and muscle. Yet it is but the beauty of promise. In it there is uncertainty and the risk of failure. There is also a beauty of old age, rarer but more satisfying. Nor does it lie only in the dignified mien and the snow-crowned head. It is the beauty of work well done ; of life well lived ; when all is safe. That beauty cannot fade. It shines more and more unto the perfect day. Such beauty marked this aged man's life among us. For his work had been established upon him. His manifold activities of brain and heart had wrought a double benefit ; one of outward achievement, the other of well rounded Christian character. Life's toils and changes, under the divine discipline and by his own choices, had left in him the best and priceless product of his labors—the beauty of the Lord. He has been to us and is still in memory a revelation of what life can do for a man ; or better, what moral wealth a man can win from his life. Of his personal traits we remember to-day that gracious courtesy with which be brightened social relations. It was a courtesy marked often by a humility deeply Christian in its prompting ; and which flowed out very touchingly towards those younger or weaker than himself, whom he might easily have overborne, as some of us here could testify from grateful experience of it. He had learned, too, the law of love. His was a tender heart. Eye and voice were proof of that. You could know it, too, by his words regarding his brethren in the church, and indeed in the community at large, especially such as were in moral peril. There was frequent practical evidence of it in the aid he gave to the friendless and the struggling. Yesterday a man said to me: "We poor men have lost a good friend, 'twill be long before we see his like again." In his piety a child-like simplicity of feeling and expression was united to broad religious knowledge and settled convictions. This simplicity was frequently disclosed in our church meetings for social prayer, where he was a constant attendant and helpful participant so long as health allowed. All his utterances there came from an experience which had made trial of the life of faith and found it good. He had due regard for philosophy and theology, and was well inform-ed upon both. But religion was more to him than either. His thoughts were oftenest upon our actual needs as moral beings and God's satisfying grace. I remember that one evening our theme was that clause from the Apostle's creed: "He sitteth on the right hand of God, the Father Almighty." After others of us had spoken of the intercession of Christ, seeking far among relations, divine and human, for the meaning of the doctrine, his few gently spoken words brought the sublime truth home to our needy hearts with great, good cheer. The hand that was pierced reaches down to us in our wandering and weakness. He lifts us up and leads us to the throne of the Majestic One and says: "My Father, here is a child of Thine, he has often forgotten Thee and been heedless of Thy will; but he needs Thy forgiveness and Thy love, and he knows he needs them; put Thy hand upon his head and bless him and give him peace and teach him to be a true son in his true home." In prayer he seemed to be but lifting his face toward the Father in Heaven, with love and trust. His brief petitions came oftenest at the very close of our meet-ings, and like a real benediction sent us away with a hush in our hearts.

Mr. White was a life-long student of the Bible. He

thought one could never outgrow that book. Till a few months ago, when feebleness forbade further service, he was teacher of an adult class in the Sunday school. Here again the simplicity of his religious faith showed itself. He did not ignore the modern, critical methods of biblical study; yet he loved and taught the Bible as a book of sublime and practical religious truth, the daily bread of spiritual life. At one anniversary of our local Bible society he was asked to speak; and was not loth to do so, for he valued those occasions. But he cared to say little more than with graphic words to sketch a humble dwelling and an aged woman sitting childless and alone spelling out by dim candle light the ever new comfort of the twenty-third psalm. "That," said he, "is true religion." But he loved the book of Nature, too; and could read there clear lessons of God and of life. The physical world was to him deeply significant and sacred, as the scene of spiritual life. He looked for God's hand and voice in it. He had reverence for these Berkshire mountains. His recreation was taken among them; on foot in his athletic youth, in his carriage when age had made his body too weak a servant of his esthetic nature. "These hills," he said, "are our Jacob's ladder, leading up to God." Mr. White's broad sympathies and Christian love made him a life-long student and friend of missions, at home and abroad. He prayed with faith: "Thy kingdom come." He labored and gave as he prayed. He habitually attended the annual meetings of the American Home Missionary Society; and of the American Board of Foreign Missions, of which he was a corporate member. For years he was a leading spirit in the missionary concerts of this church. His gifts to these and other agencies of evangelism and Christian education were systematic and liberal. A touching incident of his last illness was the request that his weekly benevolent offering be sent to the church where his brethren were meeting for the worship in which he could no longer share.

For eight years our friend had been a deacon in this church. As a church officer he was faithful and wise in counsel; fond of the old ways, but never obstructive to reasonable innovation; devoted to the spiritual interests of our household of faith, and sympathetic with the needs and tastes of all; not forgetting the younger lives among us. I am sure we have all felt this church greatly blessed in having as a representative of its spirit and its mission this man "of honest report, full of the Holy Ghost and wisdom." Upon us has fallen his goodly influence, as he walked with us in the toilsome path of life, as he sat an attentive worshiper in this house of prayer, and as he reverently bore to your hands the sacramental emblems of our Saviour's love.

So in manyfold ways during this past score of years he has been bringing forth fruit in old age. But at last the weight of years has grown heavy and he rests from life's labors. Striving from his youth to lay up treasures in heaven, he found abundantly the best treasures of earth. We may count his riches in Coleridge's lines:

> These treasures (had he), love, and light,
>   And calm thoughts, regular as infant's breath;
>   And three firm friends, more sure than day and night,
>   Himself, his Maker, and the angel Death.

Yes, he had love; his love for God, his love for his fellow men,—that outflow of pure affection, which enriches the heart whence it springs; love, too, of which he was himself the object, his conscious share in the wide love of God, and the love of kindred, neighbors, beneficiaries,—

earth's sterling gold. And he had light. Where sight failed he walked by faith. To him the Sun of Righteousness had indeed risen. By that light he could discern a safe and pleasant path for his own feet. He could see, too, a sacred meaning in all life, that of the race and of individuals. So he became hopeful of moral progress; was considerate of others; and sought to adjust his own life to the sum of life about him. With love in the heart and light in the mind dwelt calm thoughts. "Let not your heart be troubled" found response in him; for he "believed in God." He was not blind to the mystery and pain and conflict and unrest abroad in the world. But he knew it to be God's world after all; and that "He maketh the wrath of men to praise Him," in the ripening of His purposes. He believed, too, that we learn our noblest songs in suffering. His, also, were "the three firm friends." Himself! He was not his own enemy. He befriended himself. From youth he had striven to give his immortal spirit a good home in a pure, sound body. A well stored mind and a sympathetic heart brought their life-long ministry to the whole man. He tried to be a faithful steward of the divine gift of a life, to make the most and best of himself; and so was his own friend till the end came. His Maker! What he would never say of himself we may say of him: "he walked with God; and he was not, for God took him." And the angel, Death! To such as he, death is no foe. It calls to life and joy celestial. He had finished his work and laid up treasures in heaven. He could call the angel *friend* and walk with him calmly towards the better country of man's true citizenship. For death is not a sleep of forgetfulness, but of refreshment. The awaking is to quickened energies and growing knowledge and likeness to Christ,—

5

"for we shall see him as he is." It is well with us to-day, even in our bereavement; for the influence and benediction of this good man abide with us. It is well with him; for his long day of toil and evening of rest bring in the eternal morning.

ADDRESS AT THE FUNERAL.

It is hard for the mind to keep a firm hold on the doctrine of immortality. When death touches us we shrink together like a sensitive plant. Invisible things, instead of crowding in to take the place of visible ones, seem as remote and as visionary as ever. The sense of interruption, of unreality, of events familiar indeed, but ill apprehended, remains with us in the presence of the dead, and our visible lives quickly close over these experiences as the waters of the ocean over the sinking sailor.

This feeling of ignorance and estrangement may be natural, but is most unspiritual and unsuitable. When one passes fitly, as our brother has passed, at the close of a long and fruitful life, into the unseen world, we would fain go with him in our thoughts and hopes, as along a familiar and cheerful path. We would feel that the harvest of life has now been safely garnered, and that we are only waiting our summons to unite in the harvest feast.

But we can not have a strong sense of things eternal without also having a constant and familiar interest in them. If our daily experiences have been of the day, they necessarily perish for the most part with the day. We are as the tree, which, at the close of the season, has dropped all its leaves, and whose naked branches must wait for the year yet remote to be clothed again.

But there are interests taking hold on eternity that run along, side by side, with our daily pursuits. If these win our attention and fill our thoughts, our lives become by their means like the car which clutches an endless cable. They at once feel a motion of a new order, and begin to obey more permanent and serviceable impulses. One of those relations most comprehensive, and at the same time near and urgent, which embrace our lives, is that of the community. The tender connections of the household pass out into it, and are in turn fed by it. By its ties, we are bound in a thousand ways to that spiritual world, that world of spirits, which is the substance of the record of human kind. The community is more comprehensive than the church. The community receives and encloses the church and waits to be leavened by it. The ultimate product of all divine grace is a kingdom, not a church but the kingdom of heaven. The kingdom of heaven is a complete community, knit in love in all its varied and ample relations, and so fulfills the fundamental, creative purpose in the mind of God. The energies which have wrought creatively in the community run back to the very beginning of events. They embrace the whole historic record. The energies which are to shape the community as it approaches its divine ideal are to reach through the entire future. Here, truly, is an endless cable in the spiritual realm. If our lives, by their labors, their aspirations, their constant forecast, are interlinked in this movement, they will have a deeper hold on eternity than on time, on the years that are forever flowing than on those now with us. The brevity of the period we occupy is, in this connection no more significant than the narrowness of the wharf from which we leave one continent, voyaging to another. The eye may and must reach backward to the farthest horizon of history to understand the nature of those influences that here and now pass under our hand, and admit of modification by us. The eye, in the clear vision of faith, must forecast the remote future to discover the ample and rewardful growth of its own immediate labors. We are not so much mortal as immortal in our lives. We stand where God stands, between an infinite past and an infinite future, helping to knit them together into His everlasting kingdom. Let these realities be to us realities all through life, deepened in their hold on the mind by many a cogent experience under them, and we shall feel, as death comes to us, that the crumbling soil has now been cleared away from the solid rock, and that our feet stand without separation on that which has all along supported them.

Our departed brother was deeply and habitually impressed and possessed by these relations which assign us a place in the ever growing purposes of God. He took a profound interest in those social and civil influences which have so long been operative on us as a nation. He felt, as a constant, stimulating sentiment, the patrimony bequeathed us, and how potential it may be, it ought to be, in all the history of the world. Scarcely another have I known who responded so certainly to any concernment of the state, any influence that was touching the progress of events in the community. Not merely did the public labors which had fallen to him lay upon him this interest, this interest came in to give breadth and insight and effectiveness to those labors. He stood between our past and future history, as a people, and strove to unite them in one worthy and continuous development toward freedom and social life. He was, what every public servant and every citizen ought to be, a builder of the public prosperity, in things at hand and in things remote. His last effort, like earlier efforts, was in the annual assembly of citizens, gathered for the choice of rulers.

My most pleasant and distinct memories of him are of his aidfullness in the cause of education in this town, of the warmth with which he resisted the sluggishness, and the force with which he exposed the parsimony, that stood in the way of our schools. He has been for years in our town-meetings an inspiration to every impulse worthy of being inspired.

One can stand pleasurably and with widened vision at this grave of our neighbor, endeared to us in so many ways, Hon. Joseph White. One can move at this burial as if keeping step with the purposes of God. Life is deepened by the experiences of the life that is ended here. The years are enriched by taking to themselves all that was most fervent, spontaneous and patriotic in the labors now closed. Our brother stands, where we would all stand, in that long file of faithful citizens whom citizenship has helped to redeem, and who have helped to redeem citizenship. We are here, not in solitude and separation, but with the worthy of our beloved land all about us, ready to receive their collective consecration to a like inheritance in the history of the nation and of mankind.

PRAYER.

Almighty and everlasting Lord, whose tender mercies are over all thy works ; whose thoughts are always thoughts of mercy to give us an expected end ; who art ever interweaving the plans and purposes, the achievements and failures of men to bring in the reign of righteousness and peace ; and who dost turn the darkest hour into the promise of eternal life, we come to Thee. We come to bless and praise Thee that Thou art glorious in counsel and excellent in working, and that we, the children of men, have such abundant reason to put our trust in the shadow of Thy wing.

And, gracious Lord, we lift up our hearts to bless Thee for the treasure that dwelleth in earthen vessels ; for the divine presence and power that has never failed from the hearts of men, since Thou didst first create the race, and especially for the company of apostles and martyrs and good men, who, since the coming of our Lord, have fought a good fight and kept the faith, and having endured as seeing Him who is invisible, have received the welcome into the larger service of Thy heavenly kingdom.

Almighty God, who seest the end from the beginning, to whom the life of each of Thy dear children is an object of loving thought, we praise Thee that Thy fatherly care and gracious guidance have directed the steps of our departed brother, and into Thy presence we come with grateful reverence for the solemn service by which we give him back to Thee. We praise Thee for the faith and patience, for the serenity and dignity of the life now ended. We praise Thee for its beneficence, its long continuance, and for its loyalty to the Divine Master who loved us and gave himself for us. We bless Thee that in all our hearts to-day rises the comforting thought that he whom we mourn has lived a pure and godly life, ever looking for the coming of our Lord and Saviour, Jesus Christ. And now that He has come and touched our friend, and beckoned him through the door which He has robbed of its terror by His own going and return; now that He who brought life and immortality to light, has led our beloved into the peace and rest of His own conquering, may we, rejoicing in the victory that overcometh, renew our allegiance to the Master, that we, too, may have an abundant entrance into Thine everlasting kingdom.

Gracious Father, we lift our voices to Thee who didst manifest Thy love in our Saviour's love, who didst in Him visit the household at Bethany and restore her support to the widow, and beseech Thee to give the consolation of Thine own presence to those who mourn and especially to her who must from this hour walk in strange solitude and grief. Let the gentleness that faith assures us marks Thy dealing with Thine own, the pity that the father has for his children be very plain to her as her steps follow her beloved. May He who leads his flock like a shepherd and carries the weary and aged like lambs i, his bosom abide with her to the end.

And for all those who have known intimately the benignity and purity and beneficence of this life, and have walked in the joyful encouragement of its light, we pray that they may turn from this hour with renewed love and faith to Him from whom has come the purity and manliness of our departed friend.

We beseech Thee, our Heavenly Father, to bless the

institutions with which our brother was so long connected. We praise Thee that in so many places in this Commonwealth to-day grateful thoughts arise to Thee for inspiration and guidance that came from him. And we beseech Thee to impart unto all those directing the counsels of the institutions which he loved the same spirit of devotion and zeal for the Master that governed him, that all these institutions may be consecrated by uplifting faith and ardent love to the service of the redeemer of men.

We ask Thy blessing upon this community, upon the aged servants of the Lord still with us, upon the pastor and officers of this church of which he was so long a member, upon all the good with whom our friend walked in loving sympathy and who shall see his face no more. And as one by one the tried and tested veterans of Thy service go over to the church triumphant, may the young be trained by wise methods and chiefly by the guidance of Thy holy spirit to take the places of those to whom rest is given that Thy kingdom may come and that our Divine Lord' may see of the travail of his soul and be satisfied. And may the wealth of all our churches and the talents of all believers be wholly consecrated to the coming of His kingdom.

Gracious Lord, in this solemn hour, in the remembrance of the brevity of life and of the misuse of our privileges and opportunities, we would praise Thee anew for the life of our Lord, for its temptations and victories, its sympathies and patience, its cross and passion, and beseech Thee to forgive us by His atoning love for our sins and wilfulness that we may be washed and cleansed and made fit for the companionship of Thy glorified saints and for the service in which misunderstandings and jealousies and

6

greed shall have no place, and we shall see, eye to eye, and know even as we are known.

And now as we wend our way to the place of the dead, let Thy holy spirit rest upon us. Repress our fears, and revive our faith, and give us Thy peace.

Our Father who art in Heaven.